I0788705

A Witch's Quickening;

Or,

The Awakening of Yvette:

A story of witchcraft

Byron Griffin

Curious Corvid
PUBLISHING

Chapter One

As the Sun sat at its zenith in the azure firmament, Yvette sat alone beneath an apple tree whilst the village children ran about playing and being free. Yvette looked on at them for a while before she grew weary of the tedium and ventured off to find for herself things with which she could alone play.

Yvette wandered through the shadows cast by the half-timber homes that had stood since Tudor's day until she passed the bounds of the village and found herself at a crossroads where she did for a while stay. There she did find a toy owl which she did from the ground force free, it having been buried deep, its taloned feet all she could see.

As Yvette spent her childhood ever as the outcast from the other children, the owl she had once found remained her solitary companion; the two spent the free hours in places such as the graveyard where silence remained unbroken, delighting in the isolation. She would read to her wooden strix oft under an apple tree's cover and would linger out in those solitary haunts until she heard resounding through the air the voice of her mother.

Yet those halcyon days of childhood freedom would be brought to an end when to consumption, she and her family did bend. She had been stricken with the pestilence first but soon her parents both succumbed; of the three only in her mother and father had the flower of death blossomed.

As the pestilence did ravage her house, she did watch in horror upon the slow waning of her kin's life, with suffering their existence with suffering rife. Like plague victims of old, they remained trapped within the walls of their home until it became their tomb. With the passing of three months, Yvette stepped foot outside, tears streaming down her face as she braved the eventide gloom only to find that her village had succumbed to doom. The pestilence had consumed all, leaving the homes of all her kin as great gravestones. Yvette set off by dawn the next day, not looking back as crows picked at the bones.

She made her way to London where she thought she could seek sanctuary and succour from her cousin. From poverty and hardship, she hoped that with his aid she would be free. She let out a sigh of relief when she stood at the door of the neoclassical building that housed her distant kin, thinking she would find only happiness within. As Yvette walked inside and found the interior barren in line with a spartan taste, her joy grew dim. She feared perhaps none lived there any longer but pushed on inside with a flicker of hope until her cousin spoke.

Knowing not who she was nor her intention, he first spoke with anger demanding her exit from his home, yet as she explained who she was, he invited her into the drawing-room in which hung one solitary picture of the Colosseum of Rome. His home, save for the picture, was of luxury entirely void, his comfort from wealth never employed.

Yvette spent the night in a bedchamber resembling a nun's cell in its quality. As she lay in the cold bed, Yvette heard the door downstairs slam shut and the sound of footsteps quickly moving closer. Affrighted, she moved an armoire against her chamber door. She heard something tumble to the floor and, though fear filled her, livening her senses, the noise she did ignore. By the light of morning, as she tread unshod from her quarters, she did see upon the floor her cousin covered in his own effluvium and bearing upon him bruises. For his sorry state her cousin did upon waking offer many excuses; to probe any further would have been useless.

The night next brought to Yvette a disturbing realisation; together the two did go to a Ball held by Lord Alphonse Morano where she was, in the manner of young women, shown off to those who would wish for her hand as part of her cousin's machination. Though a desire to see her wed was not unexpected, the whispers she heard being bandied about of her cousin were cause for concern. She did hear murmured between the inebriated aristocrats mentions that all money that falls into the hand of her kin did ever quickly burn.

She went home that night alone to her bedchamber of bare stone where she sat reading until her cousin returned with company. As she sat reading of Emily St Aubert's unfortunate circumstances, she found herself disturbed by Lucas and Lord Alphonse discussing something together eagerly. The subject which so affrighted her, which caused her such dread, was a talk of marriage to the cur; her cousin spoke of her like a piece of priceless fur, a commodity like frankincense or myrrh.

Unwilling to be bound by marriage in repayment of a debt, Yvette did resolve to free herself from such a fate. She knew it would be futile to plead thus for an alternative she had need. When she heard the pair leave the drawing-room and Lucas retire to his bedchamber, out from hers she did creep, hoping that he would remain fast asleep. Though as she stepped across the threshold she did weep. Though sad at the betrayal, she went proud as Lilith into the harshness of the outside, for like she who first rebelled, she would not be subdued as some man's bride.

Chapter Two

After months living on the streets, unshod and garbed in rags feasting on whatever she could, a young woman approached Yvette. This young woman named Ophelia helped her up and offered to take her into the care of Madame Babette. Down to Whitechapel Yvette was led through squalid streets toward a large yet dilapidated house into which many men did come and go; the sight of the men who were given to choleric humours affrighted Yvette as they drew near to the bordello.

When they reached the front steps of the forlorn House of Elysium, Ophelia bade her enter all the while assuring her she was only here as a guest. Yvette had on their walk through the smog-filled streets been filled with fear that she had become as Sade's Justine and feared she would find from hardship no rest, thus the point of being a guest was most ardently stressed. Into the house they went where they were greeted by Babette who was attired in a fashion akin to the Sun King of France yet more wildly and with the addition of ivy. Babette was drinking absinth eagerly as Ophelia introduced Yvette. To Yvette's plight she expressed much sympathy and gladly bade her take up residence in a room to the north of the house that remained forsaken having been left since Ophelia's sister had gone to sleep and never woke. Ophelia protested whilst Babette insisted that leaving it empty let the past's horrors remain, only serving to nurture pain. Thus, Yvette and Ophelia did go together to that long abandoned bedchamber moving through the smoke-filled halls through which resounded many a carnal moan. Upon arriving at the bedchamber Ophelia did leave Yvette alone.

As Yvette sat in that room with peeling burgundy wallpaper covered in arabesques and oxblood leather furniture, she lamented her former life, brought to an end by two sweeps of the Reaper's scythe.

Chapter Three

As dawn's light shone upon her face, Yvette arose from her disturbed slumber, filled as it had been with dreams of eldritch terrors and roaring thunder, she found herself overcome with hunger. Just as she was about to step forth from her chamber opened by another was the door; Yvette found herself in the presence of an elderly woman garbed in black who introduced herself as Lillian before a tonic she did pour. To Yvette, she offered the garnet drink entreating her to drink it eagerly, for she promised it would aid as a restorative, something she avowed strongly. Lillian had come to check Yvette over and make sure she was well, looking for any injury she might need to see heal. She found nothing yet Yvette did reveal to her the nightmares she had been so affrighted by causing Lillian to give her a sachet of lavender and a tincture of valerian. After sitting with Yvette, they conversed on divers subjects until they settled upon Lillian's pendant, its origins of Assyrian.

Lillian explained only that the necklace depicted a figure known as the Queen of Night, yet of other details, she would not bring to light.

After Lillian had bid her goodbye, Yvette sat alone in her bedchamber a while before deciding to explore her new home; she wandered through the halls until she came upon a young woman with red hair and dressed in the scarlet colour beloved by those ancients of Rome. The young woman introduced herself as Lily and asked Yvette if she was a new girl with Yvette responding by recounting her sad tale. Lily offered her condolences and bid Yvette to avail her in any way she needed during her stay before she bade her join in a breakfast of eggs taken from quail. The two did dine together that mourn at which point Yvette noticed a necklace round her new companion's neck which too depicted the Queen of Night, the silver shone in the morning light.

Yvette spent the day with Ophelia in the market to acquire for herself clothes as she had in her haste left most of her belongings with her cousin when she fled, thus the two bought clothes for her, favouring in colour black and red.

After the day was done and all had had their fun, the house and those therein lay in slumber. Yvette woke to the sound of a murmur. Curious as to its origin, she took a candle to go out in search of its source; as she pursued the noise it grew louder revealing itself to be a chant being recited by Lillian calling upon some ancient force. Yvette found Lillian sitting in a circle holding hands with Lily, Ophelia, and ten others around a young pregnant woman screaming in agony, until from her, blood and tissue expelled violently.

Affrighted by the scene before her, Yvette turned and to her bedchamber did return swiftly, yet seen she had been by Lily. As she lay in bed, Yvette was awoken by Lily entering her chamber who had come with an apple red. As Yvette ate the fruit Lily asked what had driven her from bed. Yvette was reluctant to admit the truth, thus Lily told her that what she saw was no thing of dread, explaining how without their aid, the woman and her child would have both been dead. She asked Yvette not to understand nor support them yet, for the sake of those they might save, to remain of the matter quiet, let not her fears cause any disquiet.

Chapter Four

The next day, Yvette made herself useful by going out in search of groceries with the secondary intention of keeping herself out of the house, for fear did burn at her inside still and she hoped that its flame would be doused. The affrighted awe inspired by the scene still lingered within, yet terrified as she was, she saw in it not the mark of sin. An inherited instinct imposed upon her rendered her unwelcoming to what she had seen yet the knowledge Lily had gifted her with of its role in the woman's salvation, she did know to be true. The virtue of witchcraft, she now knew. Yet the new faith's power was still firmly rooted in her mind, with chains of fear it did still bind. Thus, even though she understood that what happened that night was for the better, she sought to remain for a while away, getting groceries and enjoying the warmth of the day.

Keeping to herself all night, Yvette did to her chamber retire early and for guidance did pray, calling to that God of Abraham to show her the way. After, she consigned herself to sleep; as she slept she dreamed of a great cave into which she tentatively did creep. In the cave, she found herself in the presence of a woman whose feet were those of an owl and whose arms were hidden in the shadow of two great black wings. The dark woman's hands were claws with which she struck Yvette upon her left arm leaving a mark that did sting. With her screams, the cave did ring.

Then the woman did give to Yvette a cracked skull filled with blood and a ruby red apple before she bade her consume both, which she did. She felt in her every cell's growth an ecstatic feeling of galvanic force rising through and onward to her head. As the preternatural forces reached every last region of her form, Yvette awoke in bed. Whilst she stripped herself of her night attire, she found upon her left arm a mark which resembled a birthmark yet one that had not been there before. As she looked upon it, she called out to the one who stood outside her door, yet the one in question had not yet knocked, a peculiarity Yvette tried at first to ignore.

The one who came to the chamber door was Sybil who had yet to make Yvette's acquaintance, however, had a need of her she could not ignore. She bade Yvette to follow her and together they went to the chamber in which Ophelia had spent the night. As they entered, they found her bloody and battered upon the floor, and upon the bed lay dead a man from whose neck she had in self-defence taken a bite. The brute had been a client yet had wished for more than poor Ophelia was willing to give, thus he tried to take by force that which he could not have, forfeiting his right to live. Glad were they all to know of his presence they had been rid, yet his death the three knew must be hid. Thus, Yvette was sent off in search of Lillian who of such things she was known to have knowledge whilst Sybil remained by Ophelia's side to give her courage.

Yvette found Lillian in the kitchen entertaining a visitor for whom she was preparing an elixir. The visitor was a sufferer of a constant disquietude that Lillian sought to treat with a brew of lemon balm, valerian, and camomile. Yvette urged Lillian to come with her and so she bid her visitor goodbye with a friendly smile.

As they returned to the bedchamber, Lillian immediately bade them to cover the corpse in the bedsheets and to take it from there to the basement for Lilian to treat. She drew a scalpel across the sides of the legs and arms before rolling the skin up like attire, handing it to Yvette who felt from its touch an overwhelming sense of ire. As Lillian went about separating each cut of meat from the dead brute, Yvette saw in her mind a vision of the sin that saw him die. In horror at the scene, she let out a shrill cry. His evil she had seen and saw in his careful dismemberment too much kindness, thinking him fit only for a ravenous animal's carelessness. Yet the

body was with high artistry stripped,
from him every limb and member ripped.

Chapter Five

One night after having awoken from a disturbing dream, Yvette with Lillian sat in the kitchen drinking camomile and lavender tea while Yvette spoke of divers peculiarities. She told Lillian of her experience with intuition and gave an account of her vision before inquiring timidly of Lillian if a witch she be, a question which caused Lillian to let a laugh free.

"I am, my dear, indeed what might be termed a witch though I know myself to be a cunning one, yet by yer own words to ye belongs the gift. In the ancient arte, ye have an ability I can help yer lift."

"You say then that I too am a witch in possession of preternatural power, well 'tis true that I had a vision of receiving a mark at the witching hour. I awoke afterward in the morning to find upon my left arm a mark akin to those written of in the old tales; the woman made the mark upon my arm with claw-like nails."

"My dear, ye ask if I am a witch when you walk around with the mark itself. Of power, ye shall have a wealth. Yer see, the woman ye met by night was its very Queen. By the great Dark One Mother Lilith, yer have been seen."

Yvette had it explained to her that Lillian was Lilith's High Priestess and the others were members of her coven save for Babette, for she was a devotee of the God Dionysus. Yvette then broached the topic of spells and in reply Lillian told to her a fable, explaining to her occult philosophy through parable.

Chapter Six

By a hedgerow, a child was playing in one of two fields frolicking. Never did they cross the hedgerow, staying in the field that they did know.

One day as they wandered near the hedgerow, they found a tree from which was borne fruit that they did then decide to eat. Its consumption brought about limitation's defeat. Upon consuming the fruit, the child found they now wished and were able to cross over the hedgerow, and as they did, they found that their body into that of an adult did grow.

Whilst in the other field they became able to do extraordinary things; able to change their shape, grow fur, and feathery wings. They went about making merry in that fashion for a while before their attention returned to the first field.

As they looked upon the old field, they discovered that over it influence they could wield. For things that once would be confined to the mind were now manifested in the field. To the child, a new power was revealed. Over the first field, the other field reigned and those things belonging to the other had over the first dominion with that which was willed by the children being made in the other real, with their thoughts they could harm or heal.

"Yer see, my dear, the other field is the spirit world, the realm of ideas, whilst the first field is this world where those ideas are unfurled. We who are what ye call witches walk the hedge to the other where we can work our will, to heal or to kill. Yet yer see, there is nothing supernatural about it, we simply use the laws of the universe, it is not evil or perverse."

Chapter Seven

Aware of the full truth, Yvette, in light of her circumstances, sought to learn from Lillian, to gain dominion over the material realm. Thus, Lillian did begin to give her instruction in the ways of the craft. Beginning with works of protection, together they first saw to the construction of a witch's bottle.

Gathering rusted nails and old razors, Yvette placed them all in an empty jar along with her blood and urine before placing red wine and vinegar within. Prepared on a Saturday night with the Moon outside shining bright whilst Yvette recited a charm, words she said in rhyme that would see her safe from harm.

"Into this bottle, all harm shall redirect, let it deny it all effect. All malevolence meant for me shall be in this bottle consumed, let all evil meant for me be in this bottle doomed. From harm, I shall be set free. So Mote it Be."

Whilst all slumbered in their beds, Yvette wandered the dark streets of

London to St George's German Lutheran church's graveyard, where the witch's bottle she did bury deep so that the black earth would be its guard.

After this was done, she was then told a spell to be practised every day involving the lighting of a white candle and the recital of a chant; alongside the words spoken was the burning of leaves taken from a rosemary plant. No more was her instruction continued until a month had passed, when Lilian was satisfied at last. Then she taught Yvette a chant to raise power; again her instruction was stopped until she was able to recite it repeatedly for an hour.

"Yer finally did it, my dear, ye have the focus yer need and power, ye know the way to call up energy and see it flower."

After being given further tutelage in the craft, it came time for her to develop her connection to the Dark Mother, she who knows Samael as a lover. First, she was told of Lilith in Eden, of how she came to Eve as the serpent to guide her to the forbidden gnosis of the tree, how Lilith had through this act condemned as sin set Eve free. Then was addressed the darkness to which Lillian referred to nature, emphasising the cycle of life; a world without death or struggle would be with stagnation rife. Eden was described to Yvette as a gilded cage where one would live a hollow existence, only by receiving the knowledge of the fruit could humanity experience life's true essence. That the true path to divinity comes from understanding both the light and dark for creation is born from chaos and stasis; these truths, she was taught, were Lilith's gnosis.

Yvette continued her study of the Dark Mother by reading the coven's book of shadows in which had been compiled Lilith's history. From a great number of sources, Lillian had over the years pieced together Lilith's story. From her primordial furious glory as the terrifying Lilitu through to the Lilith of Judaic lore. As she sat down to study, a love grew that she could not ignore.

Then Lillian revealed to Yvette one dark Moon Lilith's enn to be chanted by night in complete darkness, not a single candle's light.

One night after having finished her chanting, Yvette retired to bed whereupon she lost herself to sleep; within the realm of dreams, she found herself beckoned once more into a cave from out which spiders did crawl and creep.

"Come in, my child, let me make your soul fierce and wild."

Lilith offered her left wrist to Yvette and bade her bite it, that she might drink the blood within. Upon drinking it, she awoke to find an owl had through the night flown in.

"Yvette, your cousin is a fiend who sought to use you like cattle to be bought and sold, to want him gone is not cruel nor cold. He sought to use his society-given power to see you to his will bent; we may be seen by society as lowly, however, we are witches too. Let us see his life be rent. You were a lamb and he was a wolf, yet now you possess the strength to be from him truly free and from the brutish men who come here protected, let us use our power to acquire for ourselves station respected."

"Lili, I think you right, for to abide by the values of the faith and state propped up by men is to do as they willed, yet we who are the daughters of Lilith have it in us to see our own desire fulfilled. The same power that gave life to the innocent lamb drives the hunger of the tiger thus we need not feel sinful in this. Let us bring to ruin that Machiavellian man with an unearthly kiss."

The coven gathered to join together under the light of a new moon on a Friday in carnal union at the midnight hour; the coven joined in ecstatic and intentioned intercourse whilst chanting to call down an ancient power. As pleasure waxed with it, so to did their power rise. At the carnal crescendo, they let out their clarion cries. Through this they called to an aspect of Lilith known as Ardat-Lili to petition her to send to Yvette's cousin a demon of sex, to cast upon him an all-consuming hex.

That night the succubus flew to the cousin's home where she appeared before him in the guise of Venus de Milo, for she was to give him an insatiable obsession. By morning's light he had for a statue a fixation. The never-ending hunger for that which he could never truly have grew into an affliction of mind that drove him to despair, thus he sought out rogues and villains in dark lairs. Until one day, for his dalliance with them in drunkenness, he would with his life pay. By a poignard, he was sent to the grave, to there forevermore lay.

"Yvette, men like him treat us as objects of sexual fascination, they dominate this world thus we must use whatever we can to acquire protection. The sins that men call unique to women that they use to cast us into the roles of villains are of their own design, for this, you need not repine."

They moved into the house of her cousin, those daughters of Lilith to each other kin now had a home for their family alone to live in. Though Babette saw to it that the coven was given money, though, with the arte, they did see to their finances through Sybil's gift of prophecy, and Lillian's herbalism and Necromancy.

However, the matter of Yvette's true initiation was the coven's main aim with her dedication to be done on Samhain night, reborn with the coming of the Celtic new year before the morning light.

In the basement of the building had been erected an altar to Lilith garbed in red cloth whilst on the wall behind it was hung her sigil, and on the altar stood her statue, bones, and grave dirt kept in the altar's purlieu. This place was kept as Lilith's abode, and for the coven, it was to the other side the straightest road. It was the tomb and it was the womb. Yvette would be named sister to Namaah, the true daughter of Lilith, reborn in the chthonic gloom.

Samhain night came and Yvette bathed in salts and oils to be cleansed before descending alone into the darkness, where she would be born to greatness. In the chthonic chamber, she took up an athame to draw in the air the pentagram thrice whilst reciting a Latin phrase, *Ave Lilith Regina Immortalis*, a call to Lilith and exclamation of praise.

Then she anointed the sigil with blood from her left hand before beginning her chant, continuing until she felt a change in the air heralding the Dark Mother's arrival; in her presence, she did linger awhile. With the waxing power in the air, Yvette knew it time to give out her clarion call, and with the ancient prayer, her voice resounded through every dark hall.

On that All Hallows Night, she did make to the ancient one, first daughter of black Earth, Queen of Sitra Ahra, a promise, a pledge to ever seek the freedom the Dark Mother herself had given and to see the throats of all who would seek to work upon her malice be riven.

Chapter Nine

In a bleak morn when the rain flowed freely from the firmament, Yvette received a letter from Babette informing her that one of her girls had succumbed to a fate most permanent. The letter entered the coven to return to the House of Elysium to perform a séance in an effort to seek out the truth, for the natural cause spoken of by the detective seemed to her lacking in proof. Thus, she bade them return into the ether a clarion call, entreating the return of Eloise's soul to find out exactly what had, in her death, played a role.

As Yvette had been reading the letter with tears flowing, Sybil had been playing a glass harmonica ceasing upon the letter's arrival at the door; Sybil came out to see Yvette with a worried countenance asking what news the letter bore. The tears fell from her and the pair went to brew tea before telling the rest of the coven, at which point they went one by one; together the coven mourned until the setting of the Sun; of joy that day they would have none.

On Saturday, under the light of a Full Moon, the House of Elysium was closed and the coven gathered in Eloise's room, which was swept clean with a silver birch broom. Then was placed into the room a table garbed in black cloth upon which sat in its central aspect a candle of black anointed with blood in a bowl of black filled with mugwort and wormwood, around which objects often used by Eloise stood. The bedchamber was cleansed by the burning of a stick-shaped bundle of juniper and then the coven joined together in a circle. A silver handbell rang thrice in Lillian's hand who then gave our prayer to the dead, words that would see the discarnate will of Eloise to them be led.

"To thee, Eloise, let this candle flame be as a beacon, may it guide thee from the shadow of death. We call thee back to use with our blood and our breath.

"O' honoured dead, we entreat thee return to us this night, guided back by black candle's light. In the name of the Ancient One, Lilith, we call to thee to be from the underworld set free. Return Eloise from death, we call thee back with our living breath."

The air grew gelid and the candle flickered heralding the arrival of Eloise's discarnate will, brought back from the beyond by esoteric skill. Lillian quieted her mind, welcoming into herself the spirit of Eloise that through her she might converse to find out by whose hand had she been sent to the hearse.

She had received a bottle of amontillado from some unknown client and upon drinking it, had found herself quite ill. She was cast into death's maw by a poisoner's skill.

Saddened by this, they bid their old friend goodbye and opened the circle before proceeding to once more cleanse the room, burning more juniper sweeping with their brooms. After which they retired in melancholic humour to the drawing-room, where they talked of the past while mourning their friend bound to the tomb.

Chapter Ten

"Eloise had the most distressing arrival in our former abode, for she was a porphyrogenite and had been raised in aid of a future marriage, a design she most fiercely railed against thus, she was cast out onto the road.

"She had been born the daughter of a Duke and had in childhood been tutored in the ways of a young lady by a harsh governess, who tolerated not any rebelliousness. Yet constantly did Eloise act defiantly; when she was meant to be sat learning to dance in the country dance, the cotillion, and the scotch reel ways, she was out running wildly about, unshod. Eloise would oft spend her time frolicking with the children of servants, playing games and working mischief, until one day her friend was accused of being a thief. Against the injustice of her father's judgment, she fought for the salvation of her friend.

"In response to her defiance, her father took to draconian measures to keep her house bound until her debut which itself was a farce as her future suitor had been long in advance arranged; her discovery of it would cause her to condemn her father publicly as deranged and be by him estranged.

"Thus, she came upon us after wandering alone through the countryside, a serpent by her side; she had met the snake by the roadside, summoned by her cries for a guide. A familiar who had hearkened to the call of our future sister. Together they came upon our former abode and did knock desperately upon the door until Babette invited them in and Eloise fell upon the floor. The journey through the cold had seen her strength with much haste wane, leaving her exhausted and in great pain.

"Now she is cast forever into death's realm cold. Eloise, amongst our number, you were ever the most bold."

As Lily ceased her reminiscing, Yvette asked of Sybil how she had come to find herself in the House of Elysium's halls, from which of the world's evils had she sought surcease within its vermillion walls.

"My story, Yvette, long before I met Babette began in the village of Yewvale where I was raised the daughter of the parish's rector, Cotton Cromwell, leaving my childhood one dominated by a dread of Hell. Beloved most by my father were the texts of the Old Testament whose words of terror brought him more succour than any mentions of kindness; ever was my father a man dire and imperious, intolerant of all reverie and in love only with sombre seriousness. It was often said of him that he was the second coming of Savonarola, he himself praising that saturnine man in the privacy of our medieval abode's solar.

"Though our home was grand in its architecture, my father saw to it that its internal aspect was of spartan quality; in matters of attire, he also retained that same sombre sensibility. Ever were we garbed in puritanical garment, save of course for his vestments.

"The days of my youth were bound to adamantine schedules according to his design, of error he was ever watchful for the slightest sign. Thus, as long as he was present within the walls of our home I had to remain in behaviour and mien pristine; in those bygone days of my childhood, I was comparable in character to Sade's Justine. My time was ever spent in the study of my Bible and in prayer, as well as performing chores in the morning air.

"One point in my life that brought me on divers occasions to err was the absence of my mother for she was not there. To one day meet her, I often recited a prayer. Yet my father was of my mother unkind, entreating silence in regard to her and striking most cruelly my back should I in that regard err. See, my dear, upon my back these scars placed upon me by his cane, at their sight return to me memories of their former pain.

"In aid of this censoring of her life, the northern wing of the house was kept locked, by strong mahogany doors it was blocked. To go beyond those doors was a desire I long ignored. Yet that would change one night as the winds did fiercely howl when into my bedchamber did fly an owl.

"Through my open window it had flown in to scratch upon the wall as if it hunted something therein. I approached the predatory avian to see it away yet as I drew close, I noticed that the section it scratched was marked out by a vague outline of some secret passage. I took it to be a sign. I thought it likely some measure placed to help hide Catholic priests during the reign of the Tudor line thus I looked for some way to open it that I might venture in, an endeavour which led me to find a hole fit for a pin. Upon the insertion of such an implement, the section of wall moved enough that I was able to open it fully, allowing me to venture in tentatively.

"The wall had granted my entry to the northern wing of the house which having been so long forsaken was an arachnidian realm filled with gossamer over which crept and crawled many a spider, a sight truly dire. Yet the owl having followed me through pushed onward through the halls and though affrighted I followed along, walking through that place in which no living human belonged.

"Through those gloomy halls, I went until I saw afore me the door to my late mother's bedchamber which I did open, a creaking resounding through the air as I did so saw the silence broken.

"I found myself growing affrighted as I looked upon a cobweb-covered wingchair, gripped by terrified apprehension as to what horror it might bare. Yet I drew close and in doing so brought to bare a nightmare made manifest, the skeleton of my mother holding a black mirror to her breast.

"I let out an affrighted gasp in awe of that dreadful sight, suffering upon my soul horror's full might now that I had brought her fate to light. Tears flowed and my throat with that clear bile did fill, in the grip of sorrow, I was held still.

"After melancholy had subsided, I found myself taken by a great compulsion to take the mirror finding it an object of fascination. Thus, I took it for myself and hid it beneath floorboards in my bedchamber that I might avoid my father's indignation.

"That night whilst I laid in slumber, I dreamed of the mirror and I in a dark smoke-filled chamber whilst a voice entreated me to look upon its surface, at which point I awoke in the midnight darkness.

"I arose from my bed and removed the floorboards to retrieve the mirror, from whose hiding place crawled out a large black spider. My compulsion was far greater than my fear of the arachnid which had decided to remain near me, thus I was unperturbed as I prised the mirror free.

"I gazed upon its obsidian surface, my eyes growing unfocused in the night's plutonian darkness. As I stood there with eyes cast upon its form, I saw in it my reflection yet after a while it underwent a macabre transformation; as I gazed a while into the darkness, I saw staring back at me the fierce visage that still bore about it an aspect of mine own image and thus appeared as a vision of tartarean transmutation.

"That first night I had been instilled with a terror which did so liven my senses as to bestow upon me the preternatural sensitivity of hearing every faint sound; although I was left possessed of affrighted temperament, I found myself to the mirror which had been the fons et origo of my fear still bound.

"In the onyx reflection, I saw depicted my mother speaking to a woman garbed only with a great serpent; next I saw a vile vision of a chthonic chamber that resembled in appearance a dreadful dungeon of the Inquisition in which my father was assailing my mother and entreating her repent. Then the vision once more shifted and I saw my mother be dragged into her bedchamber before the locking of the door, my father's wrathful countenance the last mortal face she saw.

"The last of that night's vision was an image of a book inside my mother's nightstand thus, to search for that book I then planned."

Once more I did venture tentatively into my mother's bedchamber to search out the book I had seen, looking inside her nightstand where it had been.

The nightstand was locked requiring violent force to see it rent open, that broken lock of my soul's coming transformation a token.

Knowledge of my father's malice had already in me gone to seed, yet my fear of him the book would feed. Now I shall recount to you what my mother had written which so opened my mind, of my father's attempts to control and bind.

31st of October, 1790

I have ever been the sheep and he, my shepherd for whose care of me in the ignorance of youth seemed a blessing, yet for he alone has our time been rewarding. Ever have I been loyal to his false idol, that foul being that binds and enslaves, his words espoused by knaves.

In my devotion to the morality of servitude, I longed to give him a son, and when I did fail in this, he applied his scourge whilst entreating thanks from I, his victim, whom he claimed to of sin purge. The words of his and his cassock adorned kin chains that kept my mind from resistance; as tears flowed from my eyes, I prayed to that God of Abraham that he might aid me in my compliance.

Yet no longer am I his chattel to be used according to his will. My own desire I shall fulfil for today I did stumble upon a most peculiar object like a mirror wrought from onyx, the sight of which had me transfixed.

I gazed upon it until I saw the image of my face contort into fierce countenance, resembling in form some defiant demon that would snarl at any thought of subservience. Eyes of hellfire and a mouth filled with fangs yet features that marked it as my reflection, the shadow I had sought to keep in seclusion.

As I gazed deeper into the eyes of my beast, I saw the image shown upon the mirror once more metamorphose, changing into the image of a garden most fertile into which I seemed transported after a little while. I stood then in the Garden of time, antediluvian, looking upon forgotten flora and fauna as I wandered unshod in awe at it all until upon me came the first man with desire terrible and cruel. Adam set upon me, demanding I fulfil for him my wifely duty, and yet I refused, fighting him until I was free.

Then I spoke the forbidden name of God which did cause me to sprout the wings of an owl, upon which I flew from Eden into the desert that howled. I awoke then from the reverie of the mirror emboldened for I had walked in the footsteps of Lilith and shared in her fierce spirit anathema to tyranny. Through she, I first felt true divinity.

21st of December, 1790

I tasted this night the poison of man's wrath when I spurned he who would bend me to his will, for his wish for my compliance in all endeavours I did not fulfil. Despite our babe being not one year on this Earth, he seeks to plan out her life;

upon the arrival of her sixteenth year he and the Squire seek a union of Sybil and his son which I know shall bring her strife, for he is already twelve years the elder of his wife. I was sat with those two brutes as they plotted in the drawing-room over a shared bottle of whiskey whilst I tended to sewing.

Inside my rage was seething.

I poured for myself a glass before demanding to know what they thought they were doing, entreating a surcease of their Machiavellian scheming. I would not let my daughter suffer as I, thus I spoke freely. Yet this defence of my daughter was paid for in blood as he struck me brutally.

30th of December, 1790

Though I have been spared Bedlam, they damn me as mad still for the sin of self, for they would see me consign my life to the service of their wealth and health. I find myself imprisoned in my own chambers for the great evil of wishing my daughter to be free from the asphyxiating binds placed upon me; if I am to remain for the rest of my years so trapped, I shall see to it that I swiftly die. I take now this hemlock and with it consign myself to the chaos of the void, with my final wish in this life a malediction I say now let that man be destroyed.

That was my mother's last entry after which she tasted eternity. Her words have stocked in me a blaze which would be sated by but one thing; to ensure my father's death knell ring.

Near our home grew many a yew thus I took from them their needles which I let dry for I would mix them in with his tea and they would cause him to die.

As he drank what he thought was just bergamot tea, he grew weak and complained of dizziness, yet he was overcome by an excessive living of spirit as he found terror in every noise from the night's darkness. He expelled upon himself crimson effluvium before finally letting out his last breath, cast by I into death.

As Cain was cast into the wildness for his act of fratricide, I fled into the countryside for my patricide. I dreamed each night visions of London thus in the waking world I sought it out alongside my arachnid accomplice now known to me as my familiar sent to me by Lilith, our mother. She guided me to the House of Elysium where we once lived, we all who love her.

Chapter Twelve

"How did you come to be in The House of Elysium, Lily?"

I was enthralled by an aristocratic young man, a false idol who whispered sweet lies to lead me to his bed, yet when he cast into me seed that quickened, he refused to be wed. I had no means and upon detection of my child, my parents cast me out calling me a harlot thus I had need of work and an abode, lest I be damned to poverty by the seed that man had sowed. Thus, I was led to the House of Elysium where Lillian called upon our Dark Mother to consume the babe inside me, sparing it of a life of suffering, an act which was, for me, freeing.

Chapter Thirteen

The coven had found the bottle of amontillado with which Sybil was able to receive a vision upon touching it of the man who had placed within it a poisonous tincture, of whom she then drew a picture. His image was then shown to all in the coven and then all in the bordello until eventually he was named as Alphonse Wormwood. To find him they would use a map of the country and a pendulum which led them to the Cornish village of Sulidale, from which did many a boat sail.

Together the coven did travel to that village which sat in the shadow of a ruinous Norman castle that was their quarries' abode, of this they learned in the local public house The Warty Toad. As they ordered wine, they overheard mention of a murderer hanging nearby thus, they decided to create a hand of glory to grant their vengeance. The grim talisman would grant them easy entry into the castle.

On a moonless midnight, Yvette did enter the ruinous castle's courtyard passing unhindered through its ivy-covered and crumbling archway; she wandered through the long grass of the forlorn courtyard as she pushed through the unruly flora towards the great doorway.

Guarded was the great mahogany portal by two grotesques resembling in countenance the works of Goya yet to Yvette, it was no obstacle whilst she held the hand of glory; with its power none would resist her entry. She entered unobstructed into the castle's great hall from whose vaulted ceiling did descend a cobweb-covered chandelier beneath which rats did scurry along the dust-caked floor. All concern for cleanliness Yvette's quarry had ignored.

As she moved like a phantom through the night's plutonian shadows, Yvette heard a crying resound; to seek out its origin she found herself bound. Thus, it was that she ventured up the stairs moving ever towards the sound until she found herself confronted by a door once more, yet once again such a boundary she was unable to ignore.

Yvette ventured past the door finding afore her a young woman sat up in her bed affrighted and sodden, the very image of one mare ridden. Yet Yvette was by this sight shocked for the young woman's wakefulness was of the hand of glory defiant. At first, she herself was affrighted yet curiosity piqued and she became riant.

The woman in bed was the sister of Alphonse called Alice who had awoken in terror from a dream of tartarean quality, an event she confided occurred with great regularity. As she first shed the blood of her womb, these dreams of darkness had come to her for which her brother locked her in her room, claiming that should the world ever learn of her dreams, she would be to Bedlam doomed.

"Alice, you possess not a frailty of mind nor yet even some foul curse rather a blessing, a gift whose gloriousness needs celebrating. The visions you have described are accounts of your soul's flight; your subtle aspect goes abroad by night. You are of the same blood as I, yet your brother does not simply lie; to speak of your soul's flights into Tartarus would see you cast as a madwoman, this we

cannot deny. Yet your brother is truly a
tyrant of whom we would see you be
freed, though to save you we must do one
dark deed."

Chapter Fourteen

With Alphonse no longer of concern, the castle now was Alice's abode which she did share with her newly discovered kin. Together, they would aid in the discovery of the power within.

It was made known to her that the origin of her nocturnal terror was her soul's flight from her physical aspect, not some mental ailment, as she and her brother did suspect.

"You wish me to go willingly into that place of fear, into the pit you would have me peer?"

"My dear, one must first die to be reborn, do not look upon Hell with scorn. We do indeed now cast you into your tomb for it shall be as a womb; be not afraid as we deliver your soul to Hell for in the black water of the Abyss, your soul shall bloom."

Upon the floor was drawn in red paint a sigil containing within it the name of Lilith, which was to serve as the gate to that realm in which she dwelleth. Alice lay skyclad in the centre of it whilst

Lillian anointed her with that famed mix of fat, wormwood, and nightshade, whilst they both prayed. The others set fire to mugwort, as they had been by Lillian taught. Then in unison, they began chanting and the wind outside began howling.

As Alice fell into a trance, she saw the chamber she had been in overtaken by a wave of shadow leaving her submerged in a great void, all that had been seemingly destroyed. From out of the darkness came Lilith flying upon the wings of an owl whilst great unearthly winds did fiercely howl. Upon reaching Alice, she bade her follow her further into the darkness venturing ever onward until they came upon an altar at which stood a figure whose image would have made many falter. A great, black serpent which Lilith did embrace, black venom dripping down its face.

"I bid thee child place thy arm before Samael that he might share with thee his venom for death must come that thou may be reborn, that thou may be of old skin shorn."

Heeding the Dark Mother's words, Alice let Samael plunge his fangs into her left arm, transformation heralded by pain, as the poison of God flowed into her vein. As the darkness flowed through her, her skin did slough, and out from the darkness came a beast of fear and wrath.

With tooth and nail, Alice did fight and flay the beast, whose skin she used to replace her own whilst upon its flesh she did feast.

Reborn, she awoke.

Byron Griffin is an author and poet with a penchant for the dark and macabre. Inspired principally by classic gothic works, the occult, and their devotion to Lilith, Byron has written multiple books and numerous poems.

Other Books by Byron Griffin:

The Life Principle

A Menagerie of Menace

Queen of New Babylon

Tales of Terror From The Terrible Town of Plaidum

Emily Queen of Banditti

The Briar and Other Tales of Terror: A Trove of Terrible Tales and Vile Verses

The Lilithian Verses

The Lilithian Verses Vol. 2

At The Rivers of Hell

Anastasia's Putrefaction: The Abyssal Gnosis as Received by Anastasia Abendroth

Vittoria's Epiphany: The Abyssal Gnosis as received by Vittoria Mancini

The Nightshade Queen: Letters of Vehement Eros

Adorations of Lilith the Black Madonna: Verba devotionis tenebrae matri

Devotions to Lilith

Verses of The Void

The Lilithian Litanies